A THOUSAND WISHES

A Collection of Heartwarming Tales
and
Helpful advice

Syona Nagar

Paperback ISBN: 978-93-90261-83-3

eBook ISBN: 978-93-90261-84-0

First Published in 2020

Walnut Publication (an imprint of Vyusta Ventures LLP)

#55 S/F, Panchkuian Marg, Connaught Place,

New Delhi - 110001, India

www.walnutpublication.com

To any adolescent who needs to hear this;

You are enough.

You are awesome and amazing just the way you are.

Don't underestimate yourself.

And… In the amazing words of Hannah Montana:

"This is the life…Hold on tight!"

Don't try and fit in when you were made to stand

out.

(Pretty sure I got that off a t-shirt…)

To my fellow millennials;

Chill out, we'll get through this together dude

CONTENTS

1. NORMAL YET?

"No … Don't do this, Sensei!" yelled Antlia as she punched the wall harder.

"Come on, Lia. You are a teenager. You deserve it."

"Sensei. How do you think I will be able to do it? You know me well enough to know that I am the most awkward and antisocial person ever."

"It's okay. it'll be like one of your workouts, or one of your matches."

"There is a difference, a very big difference between a karate match and a high school dance !"Antlia yelled. The board on the wall broke.

"See?" Sensei picked up the broken pieces. "If you were awkward and clumsy, you couldn't have broken a teeny-tiny board on a huge wall."

He stared at her with a convincing glare and Antlia had no option but to give in.

"Fine, I'll go." She sighed.

"Good girl." Sensei nodded, his smile hidden by his bushy moustache. "Okay, now, take a break."

Antlia saw a unrecognizable girl making her way into the dojo as she gulped her glass of water.

"Um…Can I help you ?"she asked, making her way over to the girl.

Antlia couldn't help but notice that she looked too young to be a lady and too old to be a teenage girl.

"Oh! You must be Antlia!" squealed the lady and clapped her hands. Antlia rolled her eyes at her cheerfulness and bubbly attitude.

"How does she know my name anyway?" Antlia thought out loud. She got interrupted by her Sensei.

"Lia, this is my daughter Kate. She is here to help you with your fitting-in process."

"Excuse me ? My fitting-in process ?" blinked Antlia.

"You know, the dance where you are supposed to go. The dress fittings and the makeup and hair salons."

"Excuse me ?" Antlia blurted. "I'm not doing any of those things. How is that related to me being a normal teenager ?"

"Look, it does sound stereotypical, but that wasn't my idea. Kate decided on it. Just go with it." Sensei gently patted her back. all Antlia could do was lace her fingers tightly in her hair.

"There ! Fantabulous !" squealed Kate, handing Antlia a mirror.

She almost dropped it. The girl staring back wasn't her. It was a fair-bronzed, glitter-eyed, bombshell curled, starlet. That wasn't her usual self. she felt like a whole new person. She wasn't quite sure if she liked it or not. She stood up but tripped and fell.

"Ow !"she grimaced at the wedged heels on her feet. She twisted around in her sparkly silver dress like a trapped bird.

"Hey ! Stop squirming like that ! I didn't spend three hours for nothing !"yelled Kate. She pulled her out of the room in front of her full-length mirror.

"You look pretty, Antlia."she said. "I don't know what's up with your behavior."

"It's just, it doesn't feel like myself."Antlia sniffed.

"That's okay. Learn to have an alter ego sometimes." Kate handed her a tiny clutch.

Antlia wobbled around on her heels for a few minutes when Kate came outside wearing a short poofy pink dress.

 "Nice."Antlia nodded. They stood outside waiting for their car when a shiny black limousine pulled outside Kate's driveway.

"Hey, go big or go home right ?"said Kate, noticing Antlia's confused expression.

They drove a couple of miles to a country club where the dance was being held.

"Wow, this has a red carpet and everything." murmured Antlia.

"Party of the year. You're welcome."Kate flipped her hair.

They pulled up to the parking and walked down the red carpet.

There were some other kids that Antlia recognized from her school. She walked down the carpet holding Kate's arm but tripped over a fold in the carpet and fell. Her dress tore from the side up till her mid-thigh.

A group of boys started pointing and whistling. A large crowd of people started booing and laughing at her. Kate clasped her hands on her mouth in horror.

"Antlia, are you okay ?"she asked.

Antlia got up and removed her heels. She pulled out her large hoops.

"Don't you see, Kate ? This is what I was worried about. This is just not me. I just can't do it."she cried, mascara streaking her cheeks.

She got up and ran off, the kids booing behind her.

"Really, you guys ?"Kate questioned the other kids as some of them looked at the floor, ashamed.

"Antlia, wait…"she said, before rushing after her.

Antlia sat by the fountain outside the country club garden, pulling out the grass underneath her.

"Hey," whispered Kate. "How are you doing ?"

"I'm embarrassed and I ruined the amazing dress you got made specially for me. I also made myself believe that I am a total buzzkill." Antlia said with sarcasm.

"Don't worry about the dress. In fact, I think you made quite a statement with that ripped dress. Antlia, you make bulky, robust fighters drop to their feet with your moves. You break wooden boards ! I don't think you're a buzzkill. And If anyone thinks that, they're crazy. Because, you are totally amazing." Kate nodded.

Antlia smiled, "Thanks, Kate."

"I'm sorry it got ruined. I promise, I will listen to you from now on. I will let you be you. It's all on me, Antlia." Kate sniffed sadly.

"If that's the case," Antlia wiped her tears, "I think that we can have a great time tonight."

Kate smiled, "Really ?"

"Yeah, come join me down here."Antlia pointed to the grass.

"No, thank you, I really like this dress." laughed Kate, pointing to her gown.

"So, am I normal yet ?"Antlia asked, twirling in a black short frock with roses strewn on it. She paired it with a black leather jacket and black sneakers.

"You look better than normal. You look chic!"clapped Kate.

They made their way inside the club where the lame disco balls threw a kaleidoscope of colorful pieces of light in the dim room.

A DJ table cranked up the greatest EDM hits and boys and girls danced to their hearts content or gorged on burgers, cupcakes and soda.

"You know, sometimes, it's just better to be yourself."said Antlia, grabbing Kate's arms and swinging her around the dance floor.

"Because when you're yourself, that's when you are most beautiful."completed Kate as they laughed and faded into the music and the lights.

2.CONFLICTS

"MOM ! HE'S DOING IT AGAIN !"Lyra yelled, pointing at her older brother who skipped playfully down the stairs, holding her school books in his hand.

"Please kids, don't start."huffed their mother, lugging towards the living room with two paper bags full of groceries.

"Jack, stop annoying your sister and help me carry the groceries from the car.

"Yes mom." said Jack as he tossed Lyra's schoolbooks on the kitchen table where a tall glass of juice stood.

"No !"Lyra cried as her books were soaked in orange juice.

"Why does he do this ?" cried Lyra in dismay.

"Oh, honey. He just fools around with you. You know he loves you very much." said her mom, kissing her forehead.

"I seriously doubt it." Lyra sniffed, flicking her books as drops of juice dripped from them.

"Here, I'll keep them in warm rice." said her Mom, taking the books and running towards the kitchen sink, so that the floor doesn't get all drippy.

Jack walked in with the grocery bags.

"Hey, loser." he smirked.

"Don't even talk to me."Lyra scoffed as she walked up to her room. She flopped down on her bed.

She couldn't believe her brother. He was three years older than her and much smarter and good-looking than her.

He was one of the most popular guys in the school while she was just a simple, invisible girl. But the thing that she hated most about him was that he loved to rub all of this in her face.

One time, Lyra opened the door of her room after a tiring and unbearable day at school to discover Jack, cross-legged on her bed, reading her private diary.

"Hey !" she cried, pushing him off her bed. She noticed a phone in his hand.

He was taking screenshots of her diary entries. She screeched and slapped the phone out of his hands. "Hey !" he shouted and picked up his phone.

"You leave me no choice." he said, a playfully-dangerous smile playing on his lips.

He opened their school's local gossip blog. He pressed the tiny plus button for publishing more content and attached the pictures of her diary.

"Jack, no." whispered Lyra, a tear threatening to spill out of her eyes. Jack laughed and pressed the publish button. More than a dozen people saw and commented on it instantly.

lucygoose17 : omg ! is that @lyrariversbooks' diary ?

@nick'snuggets : wait…isn't she jack rivers' sister ?

lucastothemoon: ew…this is so cringe-worthy, honestly…

lipglosslover : wow, she's a total mess.

everybodylovesphil456 : hahaha she likes the captain of the basketball team ! such a dork ! lol

Lyra's face turned red and teary as Jack read out the comments in a voice full of malice and fake-appeciation.

"Wow, kid. Thanks to me,you're viral." he put his phone in his pocket.

"How could you ?" Lyra whispered, her eyes moist and shining with tears.

"How could I not ? I mean,this is some pretty juicy stuff." Jack shrugged.

"THIS IS THE WORST THING YOU'VE EVER DONE TO ME !" screamed Lyra.

"GET OUT OF HERE ! I HATE YOU !" she yelled and threw pillows at him.

"Mom !" he yelled, dodging them. "Lyra is possessed. I told you !"

Lyra was left alone weeping.

School days after this were unimaginable.

>PRESENT DAY<

She was working very hard on her homework. (yes, the rice had worked and her books were completely dry, a little orange tinted but fine).

 She heard a loud bang downstairs. Her head jerked up and the funny clock hanging in her room screamed eight–o-clock.

Her mom, who was a nurse had gone for her usual night shift. Lyra rolled her eyes. It must be her brother, getting into his usual mischiefs.

She dreaded going downstairs and checking on the damage or *damages*.

"Jack, I swear to god…" she began, walking down the stairs. She saw Jack with six of his friends and a broken tray.

"Hey, Lyra …" Jack said, sweetly.

"Great." Lyra said, in a voice loaded with sarcasm. "I'm not staying here to clean up your mess. She reached for the front door.

"Hey, no !" yelled Jack, stopping her with a rigid arm.

"What ?" Lyra cried, losing her extreme tolerance.

"Where are you going ?" Jack asked.

"To Monica's house." Lyra shrugged, pulling off his arm and stepped out.

"Hey ! Don't you—"yelled Jack but Lyra slammed the door.

She staggered along the sidewalk, holding her sides in laughter. Jack might be better than her in almost everything, but at the end, she is more relentless.

Her friend Monica lived close by. Just crossing a small clump of trees and a main crossroad. As they lived on the outskirts of the city, there was not many houses. And the ones that were there stood in a neat little line after the mini forest. So, that meant that a complete stretch of road was completely empty, illuminated only by a dim, blinking street lamp. But Lyra knew this road too well.

She skipped faster partly because she was scared of the eerie darkness. She was well aware that her mother had not allowed her to step foot outside after darkness but she was not going back into the house and facing the wrath of her brother. She was about a hundred metres or so away from her house when she saw a dark figure creeping towards the broken street lamp.

She stopped in her tracks, trying to slowly leer away from the dark silhouette. She suddenly bumped into another one of those dark-dressed figures. She could see that both of them had dark, threatening eyes.

A dark ski mask covered their faces and they were tall and burly for the most part.

"Hey—"she cried, but her mouth was clapped shut by the man. She thrashed around in the air for a long time, as she was lifted off the ground. Her screams were muffled and there was no way that anyone could ever hear her pleas.

The other kidnapper dashed forward, armed with a huge black garbage bag. He was about to strangle her with it when suddenly…

WHAM !

He fell forward to the ground. Jack stood tall behind him. He had punched him.

"Are you okay ?" he asked

Lyra had never been more relieved. The guy holding her up dropped her and tried to assault Jack.

Three of his friends emerged from behind him. The guy knew that his plans had been foiled and ran for his life. Jack caught him and Lyra watched him in horror as he beat up the kidnappers.

She saw one of his friends typing something in his phone and within moments, the police had arrived. As they loaded the injured criminals in the van, Lyra rushed up to her brother and hugged him tightly.

"Ouch !" he fake-cried, "You almost knocked the wind out of me !"

"Why did you save me ? I thought you hated me !"Lyra cried.

"I can't hate you, Lyra. You're my little sister." he whispered, gently.

"Thanks." she murmured. "Come," he gently placed a hand on her back, "Let's go home."

"Hey, kids ! I'm home …" yelled their mother as she walked in with two taco boxes. A huge smile crept on her face after she saw a spotless place where two siblings lay asleep peacefully on a couch, sharing the same blanket as a Disney movie played on the TV.

3. TO HATERS, WITH ALL MY LOVE

"Hey !" yelled Marco, pushing Canis onto the ground.

"OW !" she cried in pain. "What is wrong with you?" She straightened her sweatshirt and picked up her books. She pressed her large forehead and pushed back her tiny mop of hair that her mother had forced her to cut into a pageboy cut.

"Where'd you get the chicken legs ?" asked a tall girl with plump lips and what looked like a tangerine color spray-tan.

"Stop messing with me, Alice. You know how I got them." Canis rolled her eyes, she tried to walk straight but tripped a little

"Don't worry, I'll help you." smiled a huge burly guy called Carlos and kicked the inside of her knee. She buckled on the ground again. She struggled to get up but her sides roared with pain as she flopped down again.

No one offered to help, instead, Alice took out a makeup wipe from her purse and dabbed it around her face until it was dirty with the tan and makeup. She threw it on top of Canis' face.

"Here, borrow some of my beauty, you'll need it." she smirked. Marco, Carlos and a huge crowd of freshman roared with laughter.

Canis stood up, rubbed her sides and grimaced at them. She ran across the hallway and fled straight into the bathroom. She stopped at the sink, glancing up at her reflection. Her large forehead shone, pasty in the white neon lights. Her brown eyes blurred with tears.

"Why, why me ?"she asked herself,softly. "If they can't accept me, I'll change."she said to herself, determination clouded in her voice.

"Canis, honey the doctor has told you not to do all of this. You can get sick again." her mother shouted, coming down the stairs.

"Mom, this is fine. it's just a little bit of dressing." said Canis,standing in a wig, super-tight jeans and a tank top. Her bony arms poked from the sleeves. "You call that a little bit of dressing ?" sighed her mom, as she rubbed her temples in frustration and disappeared in the kitchen.

Canis pulled out a stick of lipstick and applied it, along with makeup for her entire face, intentionally covering her crow's feet and the shriveled skin, that is supposed to be one of the side-effects of Fanconi anemia.

Syon

"Now, may be I won't get bullied as much."sighed Canis, as she struggled to walk in the uncomfortable jeans.

A blur.

All she could remember was a blur. A blur of events, all murky beneath her mind.

She remembered going to school, dressed all stupid. She remembered feeling a tingly sensation on her cheeks. She remembered feeling a sharp pain in her stomach and thighs. She remembered collapsing into the floor, by her lockers.

She could still, faintly see the janitor drop his broomstick and rush help her up.

And the rest is a mess of thoughts and memories. She woke up in a hospital room, her elbows hurting from the IV injection and her skin feeling powdery and sensitive ; like a newborn baby. A small bottle full of saline stood above her.

She could feel the sudden push of the liquid in her skin, that was pumped in her body. Her head felt odd and exposed. She struggled to run her hand over it and discovered that she was bald.

"No !" she cried, but her voice wouldn't come out more than a murmur.

Her mom dozed off in the seat nearby her bed.

"M-mom ?" her voice came out a weak whisper.

"Oh, Canis ..." her mother's eyes flickered open as she held Canis's hand.

"What happened mom ?" she asked, crying.

"You had a heart attack, from anxiety, and partially from being uncomfortable." her mom replied

"Th-The makeup ?" whispered Canis. A tall, scruffy guy in a white coat came in.

"Hello, Canis." he smiled, touching her forhead. "I hope you're feeling better now.

"Yes, Doctor Edinburg." Canis said.

"I can't believe you disobeyed me, Canis." the doctor shook his head. "I told you to keep your body as plain and untouched as possible. I told you to keep your face and mind clean.

How come did we find you in the most uncomfortable clothes possible, covered in layers of makeup and a wig ?"he asked, throwing his hands up.

"I-I get bullied in school for having cancer." Canis admitted, starting to tear up again.

"What !"her mom cried, "How come I don't know about this ?"

"Mom..." Canis said, then turned to the doctor "They tease me for being ugly and all plain. So, I decided to be like them."

Doctor Edinburg thought for a moment and then turned to her mom.

"Mrs. Jose, can you give us some privacy for a moment ?" he asked.

"Canis, honey. I'm waiting right outside. And please talk to me later."she wept, letting go of her hand and grabbing her small handbag. After she left, the doctor sat on Canis' bed.

"Canis, look. I admire all your bravery and I am very proud of you. You're one of the most strongest people that I know of.

Being influenced by bullies is not something I expected you to do. Now, are you going to handle the situation like the mature girl you are ? or will we find you in this hospital again, arriving unconscious in a janitor's cart ?"asked her Doctor.

"I don't think I should handle this. I can manage everything."said Canis.

"DO YOU WANT TO DIE ?"asked the doctor, in a firm tone.

"What are you saying ?"she blinked.

"See, all this ?"asked the doctor, pointing at the IV machines and the blue tubes. "You had a close call Canis."he said and stood up and left.

Canis licked her lips, thinking fast and hard. She pressed the button to call the nurse and I asked for a piece of paper and a pencil. She was writing a letter.

DEAR PEOPLE OF KNIGHTWOOD HIGH,

Hi, I'm Canis Jose. You know, the girl with the huge forehead the stick-arms and legs and the wispy hair? Yep, that's me. Many of you don't like me. Actually, all of you don't like me. Even though I never knew why. Is it because of my friendly personality? or the fact that I would never hurt a fly? Or the fact that I've had to grow up with cancer and a single parent when I was a baby? You probably don't know about that.

Here's the thing. Most of you, especially, you Alice. Don't understand what I go through every single day. I have to make sure that I look pretty, in order to match up with YOUR expectations. But enough of that now. I realized that I don't have much time left. It is pretty hard to beat Faconi Anemia and I don't think I will be able to. Not with the type of struggles that I go through in school. I put on loads of makeup and a tank top to school today, as if I thought that it would solve my problems. I had a cancer attack at school because of that. I literally almost escaped death, well that's what the doctor says.

I'm not saying that you guys should show me sympathy or pity me, no. Pity is not what I seek. All I want is for you guys to just try a teensy-weensy bit to be nicer to me. Or at least not push me to the ground at least. (wink)

Please, guys. Make my last days happy and joyful. I promise I wouldn't disappoint you with my presence. I've never done that, intentionally.

Oh, boy. Tears coming up.

Thanks for understanding me.

To my Haters, with love.

The misunderstood girl

"Canis, You have another parcel!"

"And this one, is from Marco Presley." said the nurse as she placed a huge bundle of peonies by the bed, amongst piles and piles of other flowers and stuffed animals.

4. SERIOUS

"Okay, class."Mr. Hunter smiled, banging a bundle of papers on his desk. "I checked your tests and here are the results. A lot of you have done well, to be honest." he slapped the paper on every students' desk, peering at their faces for the sign of disappointment or nervousness.

Diana shut her eyes and prayed god into bribing her into a good grade. She looked down and saw her grade. There was just one ugly letter

F

"This is stupid, Diana."cried her best friend, Olivia, trying to hide her A+ so that Diana won't feel bad.

"I mean, you so deserve a C+"

"I-I don't understand." whispered Diana, looking back at her paper, filled with red marks.

"Mr. Hunter." she said, firmly. Mr. Hunter turned and warmly smiled and came up to her.

"You failed me."she said.

"Well…see…your work isn't really up to the mark." he stammered.

"No, you failed me. You don't want to teach me." she interrupted him.

"It's not that I don't want to teach you anymore, Diana. I just think, you need room for improvement." he said, calmly.

"You just don't get it ..." Diana softly whimpered.

"Are you sure, you're okay ?"asked Olivia, patting her friend's back after the class.

"Yeah … I'm totally fine." Diana gritted her teeth. She slammed her locker shut and the noise made a scrawny junior fall off the stairs.

"No, You're not fine and I can see that." said Olivia firmly.

"I don't think I'm going to come to school tomorrow." said Diana, biting her lip.

"What ? Why ?"

"What's the point of all that, at the end, I'm just labelled one thing, a failure. An F person." she said, her voice cracking a bit.

"Well that's because you don't pay attention." said Olivia.

"How could you say that ?"asked Diana, pretending to be hurt.

"You have mastered the art of sleeping with your eyes open." said Olivia, giving her a subtle, playful look.

That made Diana laugh.

"I'm going to miss you." she said, hugging Olivia tightly.

"You see me everyday." quipped Olivia, freeing herself from her grasp.

"Didn't you hear me ?" asked Diana, grabbing her backpack and stuffing the contents of her locker in it.

"I'm not coming to school tomorrow." she had a serious look on her face.

"Wait, you're kidding, right ?" asked Olivia, as Diana walked off.

"Diana, you know how hard it is to find a good and affordable college education these days. What are we going to do if you have grades like these ?"

"I have honestly given up on this girl,"

"She can't manage studying in 10th grade, how is she going to manage studying for universities and how is she going to get a job ?"

Diana looked down in embarrassment as her parents ranted about her grades on and on.

"Okay, guys. I'm trying. It's hard. I just can't concentrate for too long." she said, frustrated.

"That's it. No music and no TV till your grades improve." declared her dad, getting up from the sofa and slamming his newspaper on the table.

"NO !"cried Diana, looking at her mom.

"He's right. this is distracting you. The more you stay away from it, the better." she said, looking back in her phone.

"They took TV away ?" asked Olivia, on the phone.

"Yeah. And you're not allowed to come over anymore." said Diana, falling into her bed.

"That stinks." sniffed Olivia.

"I need to work on my grades, but all Mr. Hunter does is make fun of me by giving me an F all the time." sighed Diana.

"He doesn't. He's your teacher and he will always be there for you." said Olivia.

"Oh really ? How can you be so sure ?" asked Diana, getting a little mad at her friend.

"Open your door." said Olivia.

"What ?" asked Diana.

"Open the door, Diana."

She cut the line and rushed down the stairs. She pulled open the door and gasped.

"Mr. Hunter ? What are you doing here."

He didn't say a word and stepped inside her house.

"Diana ! I thought I told you, no friends over !"cried her dad, emerging from the kitchen, a bowl of cookie dough in his hand.

"Hello, sir. I'm Diana's teacher." said Mr. Hunter shaking her dad's hand.

"Would you mind if I tutor her ?"asked Mr. Hunter.

"No, not at all. Thank you sir, Thank you very much." said her dad, shaking his hand hard.

"Where do you study, Diana ?" asked Mr. Hunter, gesturing towards the living room.

"Um…the living room, I guess?" she shrugged and seated herself on one of the armchairs in the room.

"I'll get the books." she said.

"No, I'm not really here to tutor you. I'm here to tell you something." said Mr. Hunter.

"Look, if this is about my grade, I'm sorry I spoke to you like that and I am equally ashamed…" said Diana

"No, what you said Diana, it taught me a lesson.

I was too harsh on you and I didn't listen to what you had to say. I should be paying more attention to you and that's why I'm here. What I am trying to say is that you are really bright. You can do better than Olivia or any other person in your class if you tried. I don't know why you don't reach as far as your potential."

"I just don't have any interest in studies, Mr. Hunter." said Diana, frankly.

"You do. What was the topic of today's test ?" asked Mr. Hunter.

"Life of Homo Sapiens." said Diana.

"Very good ! Now, where did the first humans appear ?"

"Mr. Hunter …" Diana rolled her eyes.

"No, no no. Answer it. I know you know the answer." Mr. Hunter pushed.

"Africa." said Diana, briskly.

"Good ! Now why didn't you write that in the paper?"

"Okay, next question ;"He continued, "What was the name of the first human being to appear ?"

"Adele." said Diana.

"I-It's Adam, but close. Very close." laughed Mr. Hunter.

"What was the name of the oldest human fossil and how did she die ?"

"I don't know that, sir. Otherwise it would've been right." said Diana.

"You do."

"I'm kind of hungry and dad is about to make some cookies…"

"DIANA !"

"Okay, okay …The oldest human fossil was called Lucy Ball and she died of an aortic dissection."

"You're a stinking genius !" grinned Mr. Hunter. "How do you know that ?"

"Because I do listen to you." said Diana.

"Then what happened to you in the paper."

"I panic, okay. I panic a lot. I don't show it much as I don't want to come out as weak."she cried, slamming her face in her hands.

"What ? You think panicking is a sign of weakness?" asked Mr. Hunter, his bushy eyebrows rising in disbelief.

"I just don't want to fail, Mr. Hunter. I want to make my parents happy." said Diana, tears spilling out of her eyes.

"And I'm sure you won't fail. And make your parents happy." smiled Mr. Hunter.

"Why do you have so much faith in me ?" asked Diana.

"Because I know you can do it, I can see in your eyes that you are a bright student."

"Thanks Mr. Hunter." smiled Diana. Mr. Hunter smiled and pulled out his red pen. He turned the F into a B.

"You gave me a B ?"asked Diana, overjoyed.

"Yeah, you got most of the answers right."said Mr. Hunter.

"Diana, you want supper ?" asked her mom coming into the living room.

"Oh, hello Mr. Hunter." she smiled.

"Hello ma'am. I came to revaluate Diana's grade and she's got a B+." he winked at Diana. Her mother rushed and hugged her.

"Oh ! I'm so proud !" she cried.

"Mr. Hunter," smiled Diana, taking his arm, "Would you like some cookies ?"

"Cookies sound great." smiled Mr. Hunter as they made their way into the kitchen.

5.STRONG

I nibbled my fingers as I sat alone in my bathroom. Beads of sweat pouring down my forehead,and glistening in my hair. My fingers became tender and scrawny. I tapped my extremely short nails at the tube in my hand.

A small red plus flickered on the tube.

It felt as if a huge boulder had been dropped in my stomach.

I bit my finger and the tender skin broke, drops of blood threatening to spill.

I dumped the test in the dustbin and tore a huge wad of toilet paper. I wound it around my fingers and burst out crying.

I hugged my knees close to my chest as everything in my world became invisible and black. All that came in my head was my mom and dad's angry faces, my friends mocking and pitiful glares.

"Bella ?" cried my mother. I jumped.

"Yes, mom. Coming !" I pushed the toilet papers on the dustbin to hide the pregnancy test.

"What took you so long ?" asked her mom.

"Must be sleeping, as always." laughed my older sister, messing my hair.

"Um…I was … washroom …" I stammered.

"Is everything fine, Bella ?" asked her mom, placing her hand on my cheek.

"Yeah, yeah.", I shielded my eyes.

"Is that blood ?" her sister asked, picking up her hand.

"Jenna ! Stop !" I cried .

"What's going on, Bella ?" asked my mom.

"Nothing, okay. Nothing !" I burst out crying and ran up to my room.

I fell on my bed and soaked two pillows with my tears. I couldn't help it. My life was a complete mess. I didn't know that this would happen to me. I didn't want this to happen.

But, I was only sixteen.

Jenna, on the other hand was 21. So, even if this happened to her, mom wouldn't be an angry as she would be when she found out what I was hiding.

I heard footsteps beside me and the bed sank a little.

"Mom, go away !" I cried.

"It's me, Bella." said a voice, softly.

"Jenna ?" I whimpered. I hugged her tightly, sobbing.

What's wrong ?"she asked.

"I cant tell you." I whispered. "You would be mad at me."

"I could never be mad at you. No matter what you do, I will always forgive you and stand by your side. Now, tell me what the matter is."

"I-I'm …" I began

"What ? Gay ?" she asked.

"No…"

"Then what ?"

"I'm pregnant." I whispered, flinching and waiting for her to shout or yell.

"You're kidding, right ?" she asked, smiling a little.

I shook my head.

She froze.

"Jenna, please say something. Don't ignore me like this." I cried, tapping her arm.

"How ? I don't understand." she asked, pinching her eyebrows.

"I'm sorry. But I'm scared." I said.

"You have to tell mom."said Jenna, pushing me out of her lap.

"NO ! I CAN'T TELL MOM !" I shouted at her.

"Can't tell mom what ?" asked her dad, appearing at her doorway, home from work.

"Um…" I stammered, my heart jumped and skipped beats.

"Dad, can I see you and mom in the kitchen ?" Jenna asked firmly. I shot her a deathly look.

"Well ?" asked Dad, after they had been sitting for a while.

"I-I have to tell you something." I said.

"Yes ?"

"Do you promise you won't be mad at me ?" I asked, meekly.

"It depends." said dad.

"Um…"

"Tell him, Bella. Now or never." Jenna said, supportively from the corner of the room.

"I'm pregnant with a baby, dad." I blurted and covered my mouth.

My mom and dad's jaw dropped.

They looked at each other.

Mom's face teared up an she started crying.

"Mom…" I said, scared.

"Oh, Bella …"she cried, getting up and hugging me.

"My dad just sat there, looking at his shoes.

"You're not mad ?" I asked.

"Yes I am. You should be careful about such things at this age." said mom, patting my head.

"But, you are my child and I can't hate you for anything." said mom, smiling now.

"But, why are you being so cool about it ?" I asked.

Dad played with his hands.

"I had Jenna when I was 13." smiled her mom, sadly.

"WHAT !" cried Jenna, pretending to spit out imaginary water.

"Oh, my god ! And you had her ? Everything was fine ?" I asked her.

"Yeah …" my mom said. "What about dad ?" I asked.

"I was 15." Dad spoke after a long time.

"Okay, this is even more confusing." said Jenna.

"And you guys went to school ?" I asked.

"Yes Bella. Mistakes were made and that's okay. It's not the end of the world. You should take protective measures to prevent such things from happening. But even if they do, it's okay. You were just a little careless. You didn't commit a felony." said my Dad, managing a weak smile.

"I'll set and appointment with a gynecologist." said mom, picking up her phone.

"Dr. Virmani, Hi …" she trailed off in the other room.

Her dad finally got up and patted my arm.

"It's okay. Remember to eat well." he smiled and rushed off quickly, in the corner of her eyes, I saw a small tear sliding down his cheek.

Jenna got up and hugged me.

"See, you worried about nothing. It's okay. Just do what the doctor says and we'll be fine." she smiled

"Oh my god !"cried Nurse.

"She's beautiful." said Dr. Virmani, wrapping the baby in white towels.

I heard gasps and woke up, My insides felt hot and exhausted. My arms and legs were drowned in sweat,the hospital robes stuck to my sweaty skin. I reeked of melatonin and anesthetics. I strained my body to get up and my mom burst into the room.

"Where is my baby ?" she asked, I managed a weak laugh.

Dr. Virmani placed the baby in her arms.

"Hi, cutie. Just like her mother." said her mom, rocking the baby.

"Mrs. Fuller, we need to run some tests on Bella, clean her up and then we can call the other members in as well." smiled Nurse Violet.

"Okay, I hope you're feeling better, dear." she kissed my forehead. Dr. Virmani placed the baby in my arms.

"This is my own baby?" I murmured. I softly kissed my daughter's tiny nose.

The baby almost smiled.

6. CRAVINGS

"CARINA !" Aaron yelled, slapping her back, "Are you coming for the camping trip this weekend ?"

"Um…" Carina shrugged, pulling her Geometry book out of her locker. "I don't feel like going."

"Nonsense." Aaron waved his hand, "I'm going. And as my BFF, you have to go with me. You know, help me get girls."

"Yuck." Carina gagged. "I don't know, Aaron. I'm getting this feeling that something bad and eerie is going to happen."

"Are you scared ?" Aaron laughed. "Are you seriously scared of bears or, like ghosts ?" he started laughing uncontrollably.

"Shut up ! I'm just having this ill omen. Something bad is bound to happen. I'm just getting a really weird feeling about this." Carina said.

"Please, girl. If anything bad happens, I will always be there to protect you." said Aaron, posing like a superhero.

"I'm sure you will," laughed Carina, her light hair shaking as she did.

"So... you're coming ?" asked Aaron, his face lighting up beneath his freckles as he stared at her, hopefully.

"So, I have a turquoise bathing suit and a teal one. But both of them almost look the same, so which one should I pack ?" asked Carina, as she stared at Aaron's expressionless face on the screen of her laptop.

"Um…teal. It's totally summery. In fact, turquoise was just so last season."mocked Aaron, imitating her.

"I don't get why you're packing swimsuits. It's literally September and we're going in the middle of the forest !" he cried.

"Okay, okay. I'm just kind of excited now." smirked Carina.

"That's good. Pack up fast ! We leave tomorrow !"

The sun dawned bright and hot the next day. In spite of it being the middle of September, the weather was really warm and almost burning hot.

"I hate this kind of weather !" sulked Aaron as he pushed his bag in the trunk of the bus, his hair drenched with sweat.

"I'm just thinking, if the weather is that hot in the countryside, how hot would it be in the midst of the woods ?" asked Carina, hauling her own suitcase in as well.

"Is it too late to go back now ?" asked Aaron.

"Hey ! You were so excited about coming !"laughed Carina, slapping his back.

They piled in the bus with twenty of their classmates and five teachers and left for the woods.

They were all bifurcated into tiny wooden lodges, each with one bed and a small bathroom.

The moment they arrived, the heat had died down a bit, so the teachers decided to take them for boating in a lake nearby. Carina spaced the boating program and went to her lodge to take a bath, and to wash away all of the sweatiness on her skin.

 She pulled a few random clothes, a bath towel and went into the bathroom. Since her mother had advised her to remain safe whenever she exposed herself in public places, she carefully shielded herself with the towel and stepped into the bath.

Little did she know, a small webcam was tucked away behind the shower curtains, a small green light recording every single thing.

Carina came out of the bathroom, her hair drenched and wearing all of her clothes, she found everyone at the bonfire, some merrily singing, others stuffing their faces with biscuits and marshmallows. She caught up with Aaron as he warmed a marshmallow through a stick.

"Hey, where were you ?" asked Aaron, taking in her fresh clothes and damp hair.

"I went to take a bath." replied Carina. She tried to find a marshmallow and her eyes locked with Roland, who was staring at her creepily.

"What ?"she shrugged and he averted his eyes.

"What is that creep, Roland doing here ?"

"Because he goes to our school ?" shrugged Aaron.

"Yeah but why is he here ?" Carina asked, staring at him in malice. "Everyone knows about his reputation, everyone knows what kind of a person he is, what stuff he has done to bring disgrace to the school. But still, the teachers ignore whatever he does and he never gets punished for it." complained Carina.

"Oh, Carina ! Always so suspicious about everything! Come on, have a s'more." said Aaron.

Carina was so distracted by the warm, tasty chocolatey s'more in her mouth, she didn't see Roland, downloading a file in his phone.

After the relaxing bonfire, Carina was woken up by a chorus of screams outside her lodge. She ran out in her night-clothes only to see one of their teacher's Mrs. Polly, lying on the floor, screaming and crying. A small group of students swarmed around her, comforting her.

"Ma'am, what happened ?"she asked.

"I was in my l-lodge." stuttered Mrs. Polly, "I saw someone steal a pair of my most cherished diamond studs from the table beneath the window. I couldn't do anything about it as they disappeared in the night." she cried, tears flowing out like tiny rivulets from her eyes.

"Oh ! I'm so sorry, I'll help you find them." Carina offered, but she was pulled to the side by Aaron.

"Do you know who took the earrings ?" he asked

"No ..."

"People are suspecting that it's Roland."

"Wow, Shocking."

She rolled her eyes and went back to my lodge to finish up her sleep.

She suddenly got a text on her phone.

Tell everyone that you stole the studs. It read.

Carina's jaw dropped.

But why ? She texted back.

Do as I say, or else ...

>play video<

Carina played the video and almost dropped her phone. It was a clip of her showering. Her back was bare and visible, even though she had shielded most of her private areas, it was clearly noticeable that she was taking a bath. And it was pretty embarrassing. Her breath caught in her throat. She gulped down the wave of nausea that rose in her mouth. Someone knocked on her door. She ran to open it, thinking it would be Aaron, but it was Roland.

"What are you doing here ?" she screamed at him.

He grabbed her hand and stuffed something small and pointy in it and ran away. She uncurled her fist and say the diamond earrings.

She almost fainted. It was Roland who had taken her video !

She instantly called her mom to come and pick her up. She'd had enough of this trip. She didn't even say goodbye to Aaron. She left the studs in a small envelope by Polly's desk.

She didn't know what would happen next.

She was helpless.

Roland had this power on her.

No one knew what he would do next.

7. PART TWO OF CRAVINGS: A PRICE TO PAY

Her phone chimed.

Carina's eyes shot open in fear. Her hands inched towards the phone, that was plugged in charging. A small bead of sweat rolled down her forehead. She picked up the phone and turned it on, squeezing her eyes shut, in order to avoid glancing at the message.

It must be from him.

No, no, please no.

She forcefully opened her eyes and saw the text.

Mom : Hey honey ! I'm coming home in another hour. Food's in the fridge. Warm it up and call Aaron over if you want.

Carina slowly exhaled. It was not him, just her mom. She got up from her bed and walked down the stairs, ignoring her younger sister watching *Frozen* in full volume. She reached into the fridge for the leftover pasta and texted her best friend Aaron. He came over not too later and both of them slumped upon the kitchen table, a warm aluminium box of pasta between them.

Carina's phone chimed. Her heart skipped a beat.

It was bound to be him.

Her hands were quivering with fear as she picked up the phone and stole a glance at the notification.

Unknown : Tick tock, Carina … I'm waiting …

Her face went pale. It was him. He remembered to torture her. This had been going on for a few weeks now and Carina was sick of it. Roland had been texting her, blackmailing her into whatever he wanted.

"Is something wrong?"Aaron asked, raising his eyebrows at her.

"Uh, no."Carina, clicked her phone shut and got up from the table.

"No, something is definitely wrong."said Aaron, stopping her path and looking right at her.

"Let me go, Aaron." Carina pleaded.

"Not until you tell me what's bothering you." Aaron grabbed her wrist.

Her phone beeped again and she looked right at it, shaking.

Aaron grabbed the phone straight from her hands.

"So, what's so interesting on that phone ?" he asked, snatching it.

"NO ! GIVE IT BACK !" Carina yelled, trying to take it, but Aaron, being taller, opened it and read the messages that Roland had sent.

The phone dropped out of his hands as he turned to face her.

"Since when is he doing this to you ?"he asked, his face softening with concern.

"Since the camping trip."Carina broke into tears as she explained.

Aaron, had a plan.

He called the school authorities and showed them the text conversations as proof of how badly Roland was blackmailing her. He even contacted their local NGO about this mishap. Carina couldn't believe how brave her best friend was being. They finally ended up getting Roland expelled from school and in Juvenile Detention for two years.

The video was deleted from his phone.

8.BAD REPUTATION

"I can't believe that child !"

"What ? Did Jason do anything ?"

"Yeah, That kid is unbearable ! I don't know what to do with him, Mrs. Lancaster."

The complaints of the teachers were endless. Jason had been a very defiant kid, always talking back to figures of authority, insulting them.

The teachers were fed up of his behavior and complained about him every single day in the staff room. But Jason, was relentless and pathetic.

He never missed a chance to correct a teacher's petty mistake, or misbehave with them.

He used to stand out of the classroom every single day and never really thought of changing himself.

He didn't have any friends, as he put up such an icy glare and judging by his bad reputation in the school, not many people tend to approach him.

But he was hiding something that no one knew about, maybe because no one even tried to find out.

But Mrs. Lancaster was pretty curious about this strange boy. She tried to approach him many times but always returned with a savage insult and a disappointed face. Her mind became even more inquisitive and one day, she went up to him, and asked him;

"Hello, Jason. What bus to you go home by ?" she asked, abruptly.

"Why do you care ?" he rolled his eyes and responded.

"Because I do." she said, firmly.

"The number 4." he said.

At the boarding time, she climbed in the seat where he usually sat.

"Ma'am, I was sitting there." he firmly said.

"You could sit next to me." Mrs. Lancaster said, brightly and patted the space next to her. Jason grunted and tossed his bag onto the seat.

"So, where do you live ?" she asked, trying to make conversation.

"Wherever this bus goes." he shrugged.

"So, how are your parents ?" she inquired and felt Jason's body go tight. He didn't respond for a long time. His lips formed a thin line.

"Jason ?"she asked, shaking him gently.

"Don't touch me." he got up with his bag and went and sat somewhere else.

When he got up to leave, Mrs. Lancaster stealthily followed him to his house.

She was surprised to see the windows damaged and the lawn unmown. She peered through one of the broken windows and saw a young couple, standing five feet away from each other.

The man's fingers were curled into a tight fist and the veins in his neck were bulging. They were arguing animatedly and it seemed pretty serious.

The woman lunged forward and grabbed a small potted plant. She flung it to the floor to show her rage. She spotted Jason, sitting in the far end of the room, his head in his hands, probably sobbing.

Mrs. Lancaster gasped. It was a huge burden on a young child's mind. To see his own parents fight and abuse each other.

She made it a point to talk to Jason tomorrow.

"Are you okay, Jason ?" she asked, offering him a tissue in her office, after she'd explained the whole debacle that she witnessed yesterday.

"Um…yeah." he said, wiping down a tear, quickly.

"Listen to me. Don't hide your feelings for anything. Don't try and appear strong, when you aren't strong from the inside."

Jason meekly nodded.

"Do your best in school and one day these problems won't affect you at all, I promise." she smiled.

A small smile spread on Jason's face.

No one had ever seen him smile, ever.

That's when Mrs. Lancaster knew that she'd changed a person.

9.INSATIABLE

Leo slowly crept into the balcony, making sure to close the door behind him. His hands were shaking as he put them in his bag and pulled out a bottle of Fireball. He ducked in a corner as he drained half of the bottle, in one go.

His eyes start to burn and tear. He placed the bottle carefully on the side of the railing and grabbed his head, which felt like it might explode. Tears started flowing down his cheeks as he hid his head in his knees.

His mind felt delusional as the world around him began to swim. Everything just became a blur.

He didn't know why he did this everyday but he couldn't get out of this habit. Whenever situations became a little too tough for him to handle, he used harmful consumption as his healer.

He didn't know if it was harmful for him, because in his head, it was comforting.

He found drugs and alcohol very comforting it gave him pain, so much of pain that he forgot about the struggles in his life.

He wasn't very bright and no matter how hard he tried, he couldn't achieve good grades. He wasn't very popular and often got teased and bullied.

He always felt like it was the end of the world for him. He felt like he couldn't do anything about it. No matter how hard he tried, he couldn't get a better life. He found this the only solution.

Sometimes, his stress and anxiety would take the form of dark and twisted monsters that would haunt his sleep and make him extremely sleep deprived.

He suddenly heard his mother call him from inside the house. He stood up, unwillingly, and grabbed the empty bottle with the meager strength that was left in him.

He smashed it on an old fishbowl and crunched the remains into a corner. He dashed downstairs into his bathroom. He washed his face until it became red in order to get sober.

He popped five mints in his mouth and the strong mint stung on his tongue, but he didn't want his breath to smell of whisky.

He walked up to his mom, who was watching TV in the living room.

"When did you come home, Leo?" she asked, shutting of the TV and facing him.

"Um…about twenty minutes now." he said, looking down to hide his red eyes.

"What were you doing till now ? I have been worried sick ! Do I not deserve a check-in from my son every time he comes home ?"

"I'm sorry, mom." said Leo, meekly.

"That's it. You're grounded." she declared, switching on the TV again.

"OKAY !"Leo yelled as he stomped upstairs into his room, pushing back angry tears.

He ran into his bathroom and swept a hand on his sweaty forehead. He reached for the medicine cabinet behind the mirror and pulled out a small circular box.

He pinched his finger ad pulled out some of the anti-anxiety drug. He put it on his tongue and swallowed it with water. He gagged loudly and fell upon the floor. That made a loud noise that mad his mom show up to his door.

"LEO !" she yelled, appearing into the doorway.

"Oh, Leo…" she softly spoke, seeing her son sprawled upon the floor, a small box in his hand.

Leo blinked his red eyes as he looked up at her in fear. She came forward and swept him in a hug.

"Why are you doing this ?" she asked.

"I can't deal with life, mom. I embarrass you everyday with my bad grades and meager popularity. I seriously thought of committing suicide first…" blurted Leo, under the influence of the drug now.

"What! Are you crazy!" yelled his mom.

"I used to think that, but then I thought, even when I die, the earth is still going to rotate, the stars will rise and the sun will shine, the world will go about it's way so, why not ?"

"Don't ever say that, Leo. You may not have a special life, but you make my life special, no matter what you do." said his mom.

"We'll get through it together, okay ?" she asked

"Okay." replied Leo as he fell asleep.

AUTHOR'S NOTE

Whoo hoo! We finally made it through the end of this book. Thanks for sticking with me,dear reader. My main goal behind writing this book was helping all the teenagers like me find their true identity and advisory. So, I hope you found some great advice in there, and I hope you always chase your dreams.

Man, do I have people to thank…

Firstly, my parents for being my personal therapists and filling my house with loads of books.

Then, my amazing mentor, Mrs. Harsha Pherwani who pointed out any errors and helped me write my best on the paper.

And finally, to you, readers! for choosing this book!